Dora's Chilly Day

by Kiki Thorpe   illustrated by Steven Savitsky

Simon Spotlight/Nick Jr.

New York   London   Toronto   Sydney

Visit us at abdopublishing.com

Spotlight Library bound edition © 2007. Spotlight is a division of ABDO Publishing Company, Edina, Minnesota.

Simon Spotlight

An Imprint of Simon & Schuster Children's Publishing Division
1230 Avenue of the Americas, New York, New York 10020

ISBN-13 978-1-59961-240-9 (reinforced library bound edition)
ISBN-10 1-59961-240-2 (reinforced library bound edition)

Library of Congress Cataloging-In-Publication Data
This book was previously cataloged with the following information:
   Thorpe, Kiki
 . Dora's Chilly Day / by Kiki Thorpe ; illustrated by Steven Savitsky.
     p. cm. (Dora the Explorer ; #10)
   ISBN 0-689-86795-6
   Summary: When Dora and Boots go to get Abuela some chocolate from the Chocolate Tree, they see what their friends like to do on a chilly day.
   [1. Dora the Explorer (Fictitious character)--Juvenile fiction. 2. Travel--Juvenile fiction. .} I. Title. II. Series: Dora the Explorer ; #10.

   [Fic]--dc22
                                                        2005275636

All Spotlight books are reinforced library binding and
manufactured in the United States of America.

¡Hola! Today Boots and I are visiting *Abuela's* house.

Brrr! It's chilly today. *Abuela* is going to make a chilly day surprise! She needs milk, sugar, and chocolate . . .

Uh-oh! *Abuela* has run out of chocolate. She can't make the surprise without it!

Wait! I know where we can get some: the Chocolate Tree! Boots and I will go to the Chocolate Tree to get some chocolate for *Abuela.* Will you help us? Great!

First we'll need something to help us stay warm outside. Let's look in Backpack. Say "Backpack!"

Do you see something that will keep us warm? Right! Some mittens and hats will help us stay warm! Now we're ready to go and see our friend the Chocolate Tree.

Let's ask Map what the best way is to the Chocolate Tree.

Map says that to get to the Chocolate Tree we have to go over the Troll Bridge and through the Nutty Forest. *¡Vámonos!* Let's go!

Brrr! The wind sure is strong. What a chilly day!
Look, there's Diego. I wonder what Diego likes to do on a chilly day . . .

Diego is bringing some straw to Mama Blue Bird so she can build a nice warm nest for her Blue Bird babies. Nice work, Diego! Come on! We're almost at the Troll Bridge.

We made it to the Troll Bridge. And there's the Grumpy Old Troll. What do you think the Grumpy Old Troll likes to do on a chilly day?

The Grumpy Old Troll likes to make up new riddles! And he has a special chilly day riddle for us:

"This riddle is tricky. You'll have to think twice. When water freezes, it turns into . . ."

That's a hard one. Do you know the answer?

Ice, right! Yay! We solved the Troll's riddle. Now we can cross the Troll Bridge!

Look! There's our friend the Big Red Chicken. I wonder what the Big Red Chicken likes to do on a chilly day . . .

The Big Red Chicken is knitting a big red scarf! That will help him stay nice and warm.

Do you remember where we go next? That's right—
the Nutty Forest! *Adiós*, Big Red Chicken!

Uh-oh. That's a very mucky mud puddle. We have to cross it to get to the Nutty Forest. Do you see a way to get to the other side?

We can use those stepping-stones.
Good thinking!

Mmmm! What's that delicious smell? It's coming from Tico's Tree House!

Tico likes to bake Nutty Butter Cookies on a chilly day. And he has some cookies for us! *Gracias*, Tico. Come on, let's hurry. We're almost there!

We made it! *Hola,* Chocolate Tree! *Abuela* needs three pieces of chocolate for her surprise. Do you see three pieces?

I can't wait to see what the chilly day surprise is. Let's hurry back to *Abuela's* house. Remember to keep an eye out for Swiper. That sneaky fox will try to swipe our chocolate. If you see him, say "Swiper, no swiping!"

Hooray! We brought the chocolate home to *Abuela*. Now she can make the chilly day surprise.

Abuela taught us a special chocolate song in Spanish. While *Abuela* mixes in the chocolate, we can help her by singing. Will you sing with us? Great!

¡Bate, bate—chocolate!
¡Bate, bate—chocolate!

Abuela's chilly day surprise is hot chocolate. *¡Delicioso!* I love drinking hot chocolate on a chilly day.

What do *you* like to do on a chilly day?